D1476786

Deserts

A Level Two Reader

By Cynthia Klingel and Robert B. Noyed

The
Child's
World®

Plants and animals live in many different places. One of these places is the desert.

A desert can be very hot during the day. At night, it can get cold.

The ground is covered with sand. It is very dry. There is very little rain in a desert.

It is hard for plants, animals, and people to exist in the desert. There is very little food.

9

Some plants do live in the desert. When it rains, many desert flowers grow and blossom.

One kind of desert plant is the cactus. Its leaves are very thick. Sharp spines, like needles, grow on the plant.

Some animals have learned how to live in the desert. They include snakes that slither across the sand.

Many different lizards live in the desert. Bobcats, birds, turtles, rabbits, mice, spiders, and scorpions live there, too.

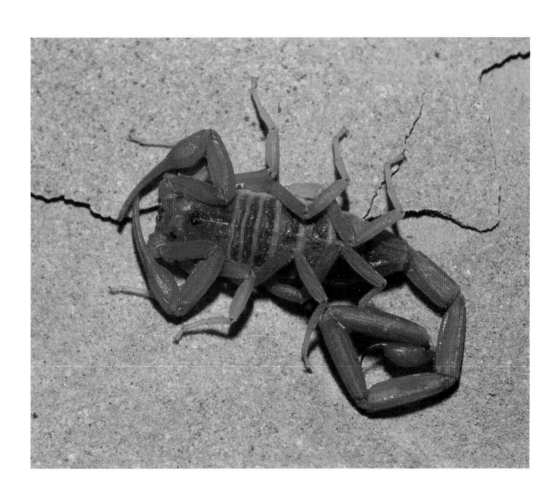

Large animals sometimes live in the desert. Camels can go for many days without food and water.

The desert is beautiful and interesting. It has unusual plants and animals that live nowhere else. It is a special place.

21

Index

To Find Out More

Books

Gibbons, Gail. *Deserts*. New York: Holiday House, 1999.

Murray, Peter. *Deserts*. Chanhassen, Minn.: The Child's World, 1997.

Simon, Seymour. *Deserts*. New York: William Morrow, 1997.

Web Sites

California Deserts
http://www.californiadesert.gov
For information about plant and animal life as well as trip-planning ideas.

Desert Life in the American Southwest
http://www.desertusa.com/life.html
To learn about various deserts and the creatures that live in them.

Note to Parents and Educators

Welcome to The Wonders of Reading™! These books provide text at three different levels for beginning readers to practice and strengthen their reading skills. In addition, the use of nonfiction text gives readers the valuable opportunity to *read to learn*, not just to learn to read.

These leveled readers allow children to choose books at their level of reading confidence and performance. Level One books offer beginning readers simple language, word choice, and sentence structure as well as a word list. Level Two books feature slightly more difficult vocabulary, longer sentences, and longer total text. In the back of each Level Two book are an index and a list of books and Web sites for finding out more information. Level Three books continue to extend word choice and length of text. In the back of each Level Three book are a glossary, an index, and a list of books and Web sites for further research.

State and national standards in reading and language arts emphasize using nonfiction at all levels of reading development. The Wonders of Reading™ books fill the historical void in nonfiction for primary grade readers with the additional benefit of a leveled text.

About the Authors

Cynthia Klingel has worked as a high school English teacher and an elementary teacher. She is currently the curriculum director for a Minnesota school district. Writing children's books is another way for her to continue her passion for sharing the written word with children. Cynthia is a frequent visitor to the children's section of bookstores and enjoys spending time with her many friends, family, and two daughters.

Robert Noyed started his career as a newspaper reporter. Since then, he has worked in communications and public relations for more than fourteen years for a Minnesota school district. He enjoys writing books for children and finds that it brings a different feeling of challenge and accomplishment from other writing projects. He is an avid reader who also enjoys music, theater, traveling, and spending time with his wife, son, and daughter.

Published by The Child's World®, Inc.
PO Box 326
Chanhassen, MN 55317-0326
800-599-READ
www.childsworld.com

Photo Credits
© 2002 Chris Noble/Stone: 18
© 2002 Chris Simpson/Stone: 5
© Dave Watts/Tom Stack & Associates: 21
© 2002 Jack Dykinga/Stone: cover
© 2002 John Chard/Stone: 2
© 1994 John Gerlach/Dembinsky Photo Assoc. Inc.: 9
© 2002 Paul Chesley/Stone: 6, 14
© 1994 Rod Planck/Dembinsky Photo Assoc. Inc.: 17
© 1992 Stan Osolinski/Dembinsky Photo Assoc. Inc.: 10
© 2000 Willard Clay/Dembinsky Photo Assoc. Inc.: 13

Project Coordination: Editorial Directions, Inc.
Photo Research: Alice K. Flanagan

Library of Congress Cataloging-in-Publication Data
Klingel, Cynthia Fitterer.
Deserts / by Cynthia Klingel and Robert B. Noyed.
    p. cm.
ISBN 1-56766-972-7 (lib. bdg. : alk. paper)
1. Desert biology—Juvenile literature. 2. Deserts—Juvenile literature.
[1. Desert biology. 2. Deserts.]   I. Noyed, Robert B. II. Title.
QH88 .K48 2001
578.754—dc21
                        00-013178

24